A Pet to Play With

by Katie Dale and Amy Husband

FRANKLIN WATTS

LONDON•SYDNEY

Raj looked at the lizard.

"This lizard will not play with me," he said.

3

Raj looked at the fish.

"This fish will not play with me," he said.

Raj looked at the tortoise.

"This tortoise will not play with me," he said.

Raj looked at the snake.

"This snake will not play with me," he said.

9

Raj looked at the spider.

"This spider will not play with me," he said.

11

Raj looked at the parrot.

"This parrot will not play with me," he said.

Raj looked at the hamster.

"This hamster will not play with me," he said.

15

Raj looked at the rabbit.

"This rabbit will play
with me," he said.

17

18

19

Story trail

Start at the beginning of the story trail. Ask your child to retell the story in their own words, pointing to each picture in turn to recall the sequence of events.

Start

Independent Reading

This series is designed to provide an opportunity for your child to read on their own. These notes are written for you to help your child choose a book and to read it independently.

In school, your child's teacher will often be using reading books which have been banded to support the process of learning to read. Use the book band colour your child is reading in school to help you make a good choice. *A Pet to Play With* is a good choice for children reading at Red Band in their classroom to read independently.

The aim of independent reading is to read this book with ease, so that your child enjoys the story and relates it to their own experiences.

About the book

In this story, Raj is eager to choose a new pet. But he has trouble finding one that wants to play!

Before reading

Help your child to learn how to make good choices by asking: "Why did you choose this book? Why do you think you will enjoy it?" Support your child to think about what they already know about the story context. Look at the cover together and ask: "What do you think the story will be about?" Read the title aloud and ask: "How will Raj choose a pet?"

Remind your child that they can try to sound out the letters to make a word if they get stuck.

Decide together whether your child will read the story independently or read it aloud to you. When books are short, as at Red Band, your child may wish to do both!

During reading

If reading aloud, support your child if they hesitate or ask for help by telling the word. Remind your child of what they know and what they can do independently.

If reading to themselves, remind your child that they can come and ask for your help if stuck.

After reading

Support comprehension by asking your child to tell you about the story. Help your child think about the messages in the book that go beyond the story and ask: "Why does Raj pick a rabbit?" "What other pets might he have liked?"

Give your child a chance to respond to the story: "Did you have a favourite part? What pet would you choose?"

Use the story trail to encourage your child to retell the story in the right sequence, in their own words.

Extending learning

Help your child extend the story structure by using the same sentence pattern and adding some more elements. "I'm going to change the story to a zoo. I looked at the tiger. This tiger will not play with me. I looked at the crocodile. This crocodile will not play with me. What animal will you look at?" for example.

On a few of the pages, check your child can finger point accurately by asking them to show you how they kept their place in the print by tracking from word to word.

Help your child to use letter information by asking them to find the interest word on each page by using the first letter. For example: "Which word is 'lizard'? How did you know it was that word?"

Franklin Watts
First published in Great Britain in 2017
by The Watts Publishing Group

Copyright © The Watts Publishing Group 2017

Series Editors: Jackie Hamley and Melanie Palmer
Series Advisors: Dr Sue Bodman and Glen Franklin
Series Designer: Peter Scoulding

A CIP catalogue record for this book is
available from the British Library.

ISBN 978 1 4451 5461 9 (hbk)
ISBN 978 1 4451 5462 6 (pbk)
ISBN 978 1 4451 6075 7 (library ebook)

Printed in China

Franklin Watts
An imprint of
Hachette Children's Group
Part of The Watts Publishing Group
Carmelite House
50 Victoria Embankment
London EC4Y 0DZ

An Hachette UK Company
www.hachette.co.uk

www.franklinwatts.co.uk

FSC
www.fsc.org
MIX
Paper from
responsible sources
FSC® C104740